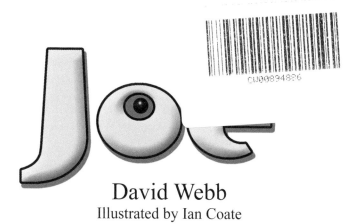

Joe

David Webb
Illustrated by Ian Coate

1

Joe, the true life adventures of a Blue-Eyed Cockatoo
Copyright © 2011 by David Webb
and Media Masters Pte. Ltd.

Published by Media Masters Pte. Ltd.
Newton Rd. PO Box 272, Singapore 912210
email: mediamasters@pacific.net.sg
        mediam@bigpond.com
Website: www.mediamasters.com.sg

First Published June 2011.

Lay-out and Design by Ian Coate.
Printed by Konway Printhouse Sdn. Bhd., Malaysia.

ISBN 978-981-08-8415-4

About This Book

This book is about a real bird called Joe. A true story, it describes the events that took place in the early 1960s. The names of people and places described are also authentic.

As explained in the epilogue at the end of the book, Joe was a member of a rare species – the Blue-eyed Cockatoo (*Cacatua ophthalmica*) – found only on the island of New Britain off the north-east coast of mainland Papua-New Guinea. As it happened, the bird's adventurous life on a large copra plantation in New Guinea was only the beginning of an even bigger adventure that would take it to the other side of the world where, in some of Europe's leading zoos, cockatoos believed to be direct descendants of Joe today continue the rare bloodline.

Acknowledgements

My thanks to Elizabeth Donald, (otherwise Bessie, Joe's best friend) who contributed to the stories of Joe's New Guinea life; to Dr Roger Wilkinson, Head of Field Conservation and Research at Chester Zoo, who readily made available records and updated information about the continuing European breeding programme; and to Camilla Forbes, whose enthusiasm for Joe's story prompted re-editing of the original manuscript for young readers. My thanks also to Ian Coate, whose illustrations are in perfect tandem with the story, and to colleagues Ian Ward and Norma Miraflor, who considered Joe's story worth publishing.

The Main Characters

Joe
The Blue-eyed Cockatoo

Bessie
Toby's Daughter

Toby
Bessie's Father

Olga
Bessie's Mother

Marus
The Old Gardener

Kamu
The Cook

Brutus
A Great Dane

Cassandra
A Great Dane

Bossboy
A German Shepherd

Whisky
A German Shepherd

Chumley
A Blue Healer

LAND OF THE BLUE-EYED COCKATOO

The northern end of the island of New Britain is a place of great natural beauty. This is the Gazelle Peninsula, where lush growth is wild and brilliant green all year round. Mountains born from volcanoes rise straight from the sea, their lower slopes covered with kunai grass six feet tall, their peaks either pointed and rocky or rounded and hollowed as still-active gases indicate more action to come.

This is the land of Joe, the Blue-eyed Cockatoo, a rare species among the bird kingdom. Joe was also different from the other birds living in the surrounding jungle because he had grown up with people. Instead of dense jungle and tree-tops, his home was a large coconut plantation on the north coast of the island, just a 15-minute flight over the hills to the town of Rabaul.

Joe's earliest memory was of smallish folk of

smooth skin and dark complexion. They were called
Chinese and they were his first adoptive family. They
lived in the town shared by other people, black and
white, who worked in shops and offices and at the
local markets. Many years before there had been a

great fight between the people of the land and others who had come in their ships and planes from across the sea, but Joe knew nothing about such things. Whatever had gone before, this was surely the most peaceful place on earth.

He did not remember his real family, somewhere out there in the jungle beyond. He felt he was lucky to be adopted at such a very early age by this family who spoke two different languages, English and Chinese.

So he learned to say a few words in Chinese, like "Ni hao and "Zaizian". Some people would laugh and say he was swearing, but that did not upset him. His folk were good people and surely would not take advantage of an innocent young bird.

The family owned a store in one of Rabaul's main shopping areas, called Chinatown, where Joe used to hang out – in a cage dangling on a chain

above the counter. It was a safe place to be, but a bit like a prison. Thankfully for Joe, this would all change after six o'clock when the store closed. Then the shopkeeper would set him free to wander the building and keep a watch-out for any intruders. It was said Joe could be heard a mile away when he became either scared or angry. But the night times were also special and much better than being shut in a cage all day. Then he would hop all over the store and inspect the cardboard boxes and paper packages, just to make sure everything was in order. Oh, yes, sometimes he would peck into one of the packages and sample the goods, just to make sure they were all right, of course. When that happened everyone was in a flap next morning, which meant poor Joe would have to spend a whole week in his cage before he was let out again. Joe hated it, but being a clever bird he soon learned to be shop-smart.

One day a man walked into the store, pointed at Joe and said to the owner: "How much do you want

for him?" The shopkeeper replied "one pound," and the next moment Joe was being carried out through the door into the bright sunshine. It's amazing how quickly life can change. Joe had thought the store would be his home forever, but he was wrong. He found it all rather confusing.

HOME AMONG THE COCONUTS

Joe's new owner was a planter called Toby. He and his wife Olga had four children and they lived at Wangaramut, the largest coconut plantation on the island.

Soon after his arrival, Joe felt very much at home. He had explored every nook of the homestead and the gardens and sheds around it   He had trodden every blade of grass, sat on every piece of furniture and skidded head-first down every groove of the home's corrugated tin roof.

The home was surrounded by paw paw trees and plants and shrubs of vivid colours. It was separated from the Pacific Ocean only by a narrow grass lawn and a beach of black, volcanic sand. Indeed, the sea was so close you could easily throw a stone into it from the front lawn.

The house was designed for comfortable, tropical living. There were no locked doors and no glass windows. Ceiling fans kept the warm air moving day and night. Instead of normal windows, there were shutters made of wood and plaited palm, which hung from hinges and were open most of the time, except when it poured with rain often late in the afternoon. A large room with bamboo chairs and small side-tables was where the family gathered to talk and read and relax. Next to it was an enclosed

veranda with a table-tennis table where the children played ping pong. Off to one side was a small dining area with a table and six chairs. In the ceiling above was a gaping hole.

The kitchen was at the other end of the building, and this was where Kamu the cook worked his magic. Kamu was a bulky, happy man with a limp who had come from the island of Bougainville to work on the plantation. He cooked all the meals and everyone

loved them. His special dish was battered whitebait, which he cooked whenever schools of the tiny fish came in towards the shore on a full moon tide. The children would go down to the beach and scoop them up in nets and take them to Kamu.

Joe had arrived at Wangaramut on a special day, the birthday of Bessie, the youngest daughter of Toby and Olga. It was a day he would not forget, as Toby carried him, still in the cage, to the front of the house. Suddenly Bessie appeared. She was a skinny little kid pushing a doll's pram. "Wow, what have you got there, Dad?" she said, leaving the pram on the pathway. "Your birthday present," Toby said with a big smile. "Happy birthday, kid."

Bessie was now seven years old. For Joe, it was the beginning of a bond that would take him through the happiest days of his life. Quickly he and Bessie became bosom pals and very soon they were inseparable friends.

"I'm going to call him Joe and he's not going to live in that cage," Bessie said as soon as she received her present. Promptly, the wire door was unfastened and a small hand pushed gently towards the bird. So he climbed aboard the extended arm, with confidence, thankfully and knowingly. How could he refuse such an offer.

"Joe" was a name he had not expected. Indeed, until that moment, he had been called many names, often, it seemed, created on the spur of the moment. But "Joe" sounded fair enough! Friendly and firm and sort of strong. And, yes, it was another word for freedom.

Joe would not forget that first meeting with Bessie. She led the way with him on her arm, chatting as if they were already old friends. "You're going to be very happy here … and there's lots of things to do," she said. "Let's go and meet the rest of the family."

As she carried him towards the front of the house, three powerful-looking creatures appeared suddenly. Each had four legs and a long tail, but one was smaller than the other two with a mottled, short-haired coat. The others had long-haired, brown coats. Joe had never seen a dog before. He would have to watch out for them.

"This is Bossboy," Bessie said, pointing to the older dog, "and that's his son Whisky." The dog with the bluish pattern was introduced as "Chum", or "Chumley". Joe later found out his full name – George Augustus Umlinstock Chomondley. A fancy name for a mighty tough-looking character.

All three dogs were more than curious about the new arrival and leapt towards him to get a closer look. Not to disappoint them, Joe puffed himself up to his fullest extent and let go a shriek loud enough to be heard by his old Chinese friends in Rabaul. The effect was immediate and pleasing. Twelve legs with three tails took off as suddenly as they had appeared, streaking in a flash of mixed colour and loose hair to somewhere behind the homestead. Their first meeting would become a long and healthy relationship – on Joe's terms!

Bessie carried him through to the back of the house where they came across two more four-legged animals, only these were real giants. Big, slobbery things with light brown coats and long tails. "This is Brutus and this is Cassandra," said Bessie, as Joe rapidly began to puff himself up again for another major shriek. The two Great Danes took one look at him and disappeared at great speed towards the beach, banging their heads on the bottom of the table-tennis table as they went. Joe wondered what else was to come?

TEA AND TOAST WITH TOBY

Joe slept his first night at Wangaramut on a beam up in the roof of the house after finding a cosy spot there. Bessie had put him there through a hole in the eaves. "You'll be safe here until we can find somewhere better," she said, standing on a wooden box to reach the hole above. Joe thought it was a great idea. He had the whole of this big space to explore without interference from nosey dogs. Bessie was right; it was protected and he was happy there.

Early next morning he woke up to the sound of many strange noises. He soon got to know them as the moo-ing of cows and the quacking of geese and ducks. Even so, on that first morning one needed to be cautious about such things.

Climbing his way down a veranda pole he spied Toby in the living room. Wearing singlet and trousers and a sturdy pair of shoes, Toby was sitting in one of the bamboo chairs looking at a large piece of paper which he held in one hand. With his other hand he was drinking from a white container. Joe felt it was a good time to say hello again. He waddled into the living room and reached the leg of Toby's chair. "Ni hao," he said at first in Chinese, then "cocky kai kai," which were the first new words he had just learnt. "Crikey," said Toby, spilling tea onto his singlet. "Is that you, Joe?"

Joe was embarrassed. Dumb bird, he thought to himself. That's not a good start to the day. But Toby was a kind man. And maybe he was a bit embarrassed, too. "How about a cuppa?" he said, pouring some of his tea from the cup into a saucer, which he put down on the floor. "And a piece of toast?" he asked, breaking off some bread from a half-eaten slice and placing it in the saucer.

It was delicious. From that moment Toby and Joe became good mates and most mornings on Wangaramut would begin with tea and toast for two.

Just then Bessie came into the room. She seemed delighted and a little surprised to see her new friend, no doubt half expecting that he would still be up in his roof hideaway. "Did you get him down?" she asked her dad. "No," came the reply. "He must have climbed down on his own ... and he just about frightened the living daylights out of me!"

Bessie lifted him up and carried him to the front of the building. Her doll's pram, crammed with bits of rag, old tins and her favourite things from here and there, was at the side of the entrance where she had left it the night before. "I'm going to show you where everything is, Joe," she said, putting him on the front of the pram where he perched facing back towards her. "Hold on," she told him.

Joe learned very quickly that it was much easier to face the direction in which he was heading when sitting on the front of the pram. And to flap his wings, his head well forward, to maintain balance and stay on course. It was also very exciting to be part of a team effort designed to go from one end of the homestead to the other in the fastest possible time. He could not recall Bessie ever walking anywhere; she always ran. There was never enough time in a day to do all the things she needed to do. Their journeys together around Wangaramut, with Bessie running at full pace and Joe spearheading the way at the bow of the pram, happened regularly, sometimes three times a day.

Bessie left Wangaramut most days soon after breakfast and then came home again in the mid-afternoon. She told Joe that she had to attend school on those days. The best days were when she stayed with him all day on the plantation. He did not know what school was, but he didn't like it.

"We are going to Rabaul tomorrow," Bessie told Joe one morning. "And you," she added, pointing at him, "are coming with me."

Well, that sounded quite promising until she brought out his old cage, which by now was showing signs of rust. "I must paint it," said Bessie, sorting through various tins in the big shed behind the homestead. She chose one and used a brush to dab paint all over the cage, changing its colour from a dirty brown to a bright green. "That will do fine," she said as she finished. "We will leave it until the morning to dry."

So much for that. Joe still did not like the cage. After all, it was Bessie who had said he would no longer have to live in it. Had she gone back on her word? That night he did not sleep well in his rooftop hideaway. But the next day everything seemed as usual. A cup of tea and toast with Toby, followed by a pram whizz around the garden and a bit of a run-in with Marus, the gardener, who was always trying to shoo him away. A silly old man, thought Joe. He could never be friends with him.

Midday came and went as usual. Just as he was wondering what fun the rest of the afternoon might bring, Bessie appeared around the corner of the living room carrying the cage, now all clean and green. "Come on Joe," she said, "we're going to Rabaul," and before he knew what was happening he was inside his old prison looking out through a green grille.

This was not good, Joe protested loudly. He may even have sworn in Chinese, because he let go all his words in one hysterical shriek. This was madness. Stuck in a cage when he had been promised and shown such freedom. His world crashed around him as he was carried protesting to the back seat of the vehicle. Now he was leaving and, horror of horrors, in a cage!

"You will be all right . . . just behave," said Bessie. Sure, Joe thought, I guess you've grown tired of me and decided to give me back to my old owners. He slumped on the lower perch in the corner and buried his head deep in his chest feathers. "Don't get down in the dumps, Joe, you're going to be a star," Bessie said. She could see all was not well with her friend.

After driving miles along the dusty road they reached Rabaul, where Toby drove the car into a large yard next to a long building. This was not Chinatown, Joe decided. But many people were there as well as many animals – dogs and ducks, even a cow and a pig and a couple of birds in cages just like Joe. His heart sank even further. Quite clearly this was a marketplace where people came to buy and sell.

They are going to get rid of me to the highest bidder, Joe thought. Once again he protested, using all his strength and wind-power in a desperate bid to escape his prison.

"Oh look at Joe, he's got green stripes all over him," Bessie shouted in shock. The paint was not quite dry. "Please Joe, just behave yourself, will you," she pleaded again.

Joe was placed on a bench alongside a wall in the yard between two other cages. In one was a small puppy dog, in the other a black parrot. A number on a round piece of paper was stuck to the front of his cage. Now he really knew he was back in prison.

People walked by and peered at him, some joking and pointing. Then after a long while a man and a woman in white coats came by and stared at him again. For several minutes they talked to each other and made marks on pieces of paper. Then they were gone. Just like that.

More time passed, more faces, more peering and then, just as he was expecting the worst, Bessie arrived. She picked up the cage and said: "Come on, Joe, it's time to go home."

As they drove from the yard Bessie said to Toby: "I think Joe would have won a prize if he had behaved normally. But he threw such a tantrum. Now look at him. I don't know how I am going to get all that green paint off him."

So they went home to Wangaramut . . . and Bessie never entered Joe in a school pets contest again.

JOE, THE STAR

As time went by, many people heard about Joe. The word got around about his funny ways and habits, and sometimes the tricks he would get up to. Friends of Olga and Toby would come to Wangaramut to watch him perform. They would bring their cameras and take pictures of him. Joe was becoming famous!

Joe would present himself regularly at meal times when everyone was seated at the dining room table. He did this in a very funny way, through a hole in the ceiling above the table. It was just large enough for Joe to poke his head through. "Cocky kai kai," he would screech, shoving his head down towards the most tasty-looking dish. Bessie's family were used to Joe appearing this way, but sometimes guests were so surprised they would choke on their food. "Go away, Joe," Olga would say to try and save the day. "You're an embarrassment." So Joe would disappear back in his safe hideaway, leaving the guests below trying to

eat their meal as if nothing had happened, but always with an eye on the hole above, just in case Joe should suddenly come back.

Joe's star performance was at the wedding of one of Toby's best friends, and everyone was taken by surprise this time, including Toby. The wedding was held one evening on the front lawn of Wangaramut, a perfect tropical setting all lit up by fairy lights. The ceremony went as planned until, just as the bride and groom were being asked to make their vows, all the lights went out. Poor Toby asked everyone to be patient while he sorted out the embarrassing problem. Clearly a fuse had blown, he thought, making his way with great difficulty in the dark to the fuse box at the back of the house. He soon discovered exactly what was wrong. The door of the fuse box was open and all the fuses had been taken out and scattered on the floor beneath it. And there, on top of the fuse box sat Joe, who greeted Toby with a rather sheepish "cocky kai

kai". Toby shook his head in disbelief, but he could not get angry with him. Instead, he just smiled as he put the fuses back in place, one by one, picked up Joe and went back to the wedding guests.

Only a bird like Joe could steal the limelight from the bride and groom on their wedding day, even if it was just for ten minutes. That night he slept soundly in the roof of the house, pleased with his day's efforts. He didn't even hear the noisy wedding guests beneath him as the party went on into the early hours of the next day.

JOE GOES MISSING

Wangaramut was always on the move with many people. There was Kamu, the cook, who was fair and generous towards Joe. When Bessie was at school Joe would usually find his way to Kamu for a chat and some "kai kai", the magic words for all kinds of treats. Kamu enjoyed having his company. "Hello, Joe, cocky kai kai," he would say, slipping the bird some battered whitebait left over from last night's dinner.

But Joe and the old gardener, Marus, were not on such good terms. Maybe he should stay right away from his garden, Joe thought. Or at least stop digging up the tasty

roots under the soil. Was that why the old man did not like him? Or was it because when Joe called out at night sometimes it sounded like one of the hens the old man looked after. The silly hens were locked inside a wire pen at night to keep them safe. When Joe made his own cackling sound, the old man would come hurrying out looking for a hen, only to find it was Joe making the noise. Then he would get very angry and go back into his little house, slamming the door behind him.

Many other people worked on the plantation. They lived in small houses made of bamboo and straw not far from the main homestead. Like Kamu and Marus, these workers also wore short cloth skirts, called lap-laps, around their waists. Their feet were always bare and they spoke a strange language Joe had not heard before. Many of them chewed nuts mixed with a white powder which made their teeth and mouths red. Some of them also carried big knives for gathering coconuts from the tall palms. They did not seem very friendly.

So Joe learned to be wary of these people and stay a safe distance from them. Best keep to his own patch close to the homestead. That way he could avoid any trouble. At least, that's what he hoped.

One morning Joe disappeared. There was no early bird to join Toby in a morning cup of tea. No squawking "cocky kai kai" to rouse the sleeping dogs and annoy the gardener. Worst of all, Bessie's new friend had just vanished into thin air.

Had he discovered his wings and flown away? Or gone for a walk in the jungle and lost his way? Everyone was upset and worried. Bessie was beside herself and would not be comforted. "Where are you, Joe?" she cried, hoping he might suddenly fly down from the sky. Toby and Olga were just as upset.

A week passed and there was still no clue where he was. Every corner of the homestead had been searched. But no sign of Joe. Olga had put the word around among the people on the plantation. Maybe one of them knew where Joe was, or if he had been stolen by someone.

Another week went by and there was still no news. Then one morning, a young boy who sometimes worked with Kamu, helping him in the kitchen, came to Olga. He seemed very excited, pointing his arm towards the distant hills. "You lookim Joe, you lookim Joe," he said in Pidgin English, and Olga nodded. She understood what he meant. Someone had told the young lad that Joe had been taken in the direction where he was pointing?

"You show me the way," she said to him, as they walked towards her car. She and the boy would go alone. Bessie was at school and Toby was busy with work.

They drove along a dusty dirt road towards the hills. As they got closer, the boy began to talk again, saying "slow, slow" to Olga, as she drove around a bend in the road. "Stop here," the boy commanded when the car reached a narrow track on the side of the road. She stopped the car and they got out.

The track led through the jungle to a small village. It was not a long way and when the village suddenly came in view, the boy told Olga: "Wait here."

It was not a long wait. Just minutes after he left he was back again, this time with two other people from the village. One of them, a small woman, was carrying something in her arms, covered by a piece of cloth. The woman looked up at Olga and asked: "This yours?" Olga lifted the cloth and there, sure enough, was Joe. "Yes, he is," said Olga, overjoyed at seeing him again. The woman handed him to Olga and he quickly snuggled close to her. Then came a barely audible "cocky kai kai".

The bird was Joe, all right, but he was dirty and scruffy and he looked a bit sad. Olga carried him back to the car and took him home – and there was much rejoicing.

The reason for Joe's sudden disappearance would remain a mystery, although it seemed clear someone had taken him from the plantation to the village. Someone who didn't like the bird, or someone who wanted him as a pet? Whatever the reason, his sudden departure from Wangaramut made little sense. The young lad who had shown Olga to the village could only say that the word had been passed around about Joe's whereabouts on the jungle grapevine.

Back in his familiar surroundings again, Joe took a while to regain his appetite and sense of fun. With Bessie's love and care his confidence returned. Soon, it was as if he had never been away.

He was happy again!

JOE FINDS HIS WINGS

Joe had never really thought about flying. As a young bird he had spent all his time with his feet firmly on the ground. And why not? Everyone else he knew walked or ran, so why should he be any different? He had been brought up in a store and spent much of his time in a cage, and so he had got used to being carried from place to place. Then there were the times he travelled in Toby's car, or got around perched on the front of Bessie's pram. The most he ever did was sometimes flap his wings, because somehow it seemed the natural thing to do.

That all changed one day at Wangaramut, the day he had his first meeting with a snake. It was a giant python that suddenly appeared without any warning next to the front gate. Joe thought it looked really evil, a monster with a body that went on forever and eyes that stared at him without so much as a blink. As it moved closer to him Joe considered his chances and decided this was not the time to puff up his neck feathers and shriek. What worked for the dogs did not seem likely to work with this thing. Why run the risk, anyway!

So he turned and ran away from the gate back towards the house, frantically flapping his wings. And as he ran, the air seemed to gather from beneath his body and push him upwards. Harder, harder, harder he worked his wings. His feet were still moving but were no longer touching the ground. He was treading air. Yes, he was flying!

He was panting for breath as he clung to the gutter of the roof. What a wonderful feeling!

Looking down, Joe had a splendid view of the lawn where he had been less than a minute before. There was no longer any sign of the giant snake. It had probably moved off to look for other food. The danger was gone. But what could he do now?

If he left his position of safety, he would surely fall to the ground. Flapping his wings and flying upwards had seemed quite easy, but he wasn't so sure about flapping them to fly downwards. That did not seem to make a lot of sense. Joe decided he would need to seek some friendly help.

Just then Bessie came running out from under the eve of the house, shouting "where are you, Joe, where are you, Joe?" She stood on the lawn below and peered all around her into the deepening shadows of the oncoming night. "Joe, where are you?" she called again.

Dear Bessie had answered his call. Always, she came to help. What a true friend she was. Joe made a loud squawk, which took her completely by surprise. She spun around, looking up. "Goodness gracious, Joe, how did you get up there?" she said, a big smile on her face. She disappeared just as quickly as she had arrived, to return in a flash with Toby and Olga. "There he is, Mum," she said, pointing to Joe on the

front edge of the gutter. "He must have flown up there."

Toby said something and quickly walked back under the eve. Olga said: "He'll find a way down if you give him time." But Bessie was not happy. "Look, he's scared . . . he's got up there and doesn't know how to get back down again." What a good friend she was. She understood. It wasn't the height that worried Joe. It was the yawning depth below.

Soon Toby came back, this time carrying a long ladder, which he propped up against the gutter where the bird was standing. Then he began to climb. "Come on Joe, hop on," he said when he reached the top. Joe climbed onto the outstretched arm and moved sideways to Toby's shoulder. They then came down safely together from the roof to the ground.

For several weeks Joe practised taking off and landing. At first it didn't always work as he planned and the ladder was kept on standby to bring him down to earth from the trees and rooftops. But as he kept practising, his confidence grew and he found he could fly without any fear of falling to the ground.

He was so confident now he would fly up to the gutter

of the homestead, squawking and screeching to get everyone's attention. Then when all eyes were glued on him, he would strut to the top, turn round and rush downwards at great speed towards the gutter. He always went head first, stretching forward with his beak touching the roof to guide him down the slope. It was an amazing sight. Then just when everyone thought he would fall off the edge he would catch hold of the gutter with his claw and dangle there, screeching and flapping his wings as the people on the

ground below clapped and shouted "Well done Joe."
If they clapped long enough he might do it again.

****

Now that he could fly it was not long before Joe
decided it was time to see more of the world. He had
sometimes wondered about others like himself. Who
were his real parents, his brothers and his sisters?
Did they also live like him on plantations? Or maybe
in cages?

He might never find the answers to these worrying
questions. But maybe the sounds of the jungle all
around Wangaramut would give some clues. He
needed to find out for himself.

JOE GOES ON A MISSION

Joe took off early one morning as the sun began to rise inland. The front of the homestead was still in darkness. This morning he had not waited for his cup of tea with Toby. No doubt he would wonder where Joe was. He knew sometimes Joe would make an early morning inspection of the garden and turn up late for breakfast. Bessie had gone to stay with one of her school friends in Rabaul. She had spoken to him as she left the previous evening. "Just behave while I'm away, Joe," she said, putting him on the pram. "I'll be back tomorrow night."

With an early start and a whole day ahead of him, Joe stretched his wings and began to fly along the coastline which he was sure would take him back to the place of his birth. Five hundred feet below him was the dusty dirt road where he had travelled months ago in the back of Toby's truck - on his way to becoming a present for Bessie. He thought about

52

that as he soared higher to get a better view of the world on this brilliant new day.

Gathering more and more height, Joe was amazed at the size of the horizon. His vision was split in two; to the left an endless deep blue sea and, to the right, the many peaks and valleys of land slowly turning from brown to green. He had never flown to such heights before. He had never seen such beauty. Higher and higher Joe flew, alone in space. Now the high peaks were just two thousand feet below him. He flew over them. Maybe, he thought, I am at the top of the world.

There was no sign of other life, no other flutter of wings, just silence. For a moment he was tempted to stay there, drifting with the up-drafts of warm air and gliding in wide sweeps above all the blue and green. But he had a mission. He must keep going.

Soon the land mass to the right of him began to narrow. Now he could see two coastlines. This was the top end of the island, much of it created from noisy, volcanic eruptions. On the far side of the coastline a large bay was dotted with small fishing boats. There were also many buildings and roads and he now could see the

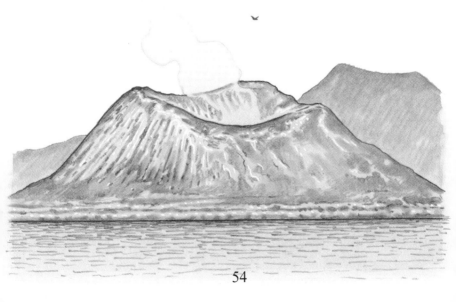

movement of vehicles and people. This must surely be the busiest place on the whole of earth. Rabaul.

Now Joe flew down towards the road, gliding over the hills in the direction of the buildings. Soon he was above the centre of the town where people were going from place to place carrying bags and goods. He quickly came to the shops of old Chinatown, where he had spent so much of his early youth. He descended lightly to the highest point of the roofline, and stayed a while. Looking down he remembered the drab look of the homes on the opposite side of the treeless street, seen from ground level through metal grilles and flywire. Nothing seemed to have changed. He wondered if there was another bird caged and hanging above the counter below where he now stood free.

It was time to move on. He took off, flying swiftly over the flat rooftops and out toward the end of the peninsula where the sea formed an inlet separating flat, green jungle and the sudden slopes of a bare volcano – a place in whose shadows Joe had been born. The smell of sulphur brought back long-ago memories of bubbling water and shaking ground. "Gurias", the people called them when the earth moved, and they looked nervously towards the volcano.

Joe flew across the narrow stretch of water to the sandy shoreline, then pushed himself higher again above the treetops. He needed to get his bearings.

Below was a village of houses made from thatch and bamboo where the local people lived. Not much further on he saw a moving flash of white among the green. And then another, and another. No doubt this was the sign of a flock of birds. Maybe his own kind? Now he was over the top of the trees and he began to fly down in big, sweeping circles. Closer and closer he flew and, suddenly, he was there. A tremendous screech came from beneath him. It seemed like a choir of a thousand birds, all in tune together This surely was a family greeting, a welcoming home.

There were hundreds or more, maybe a thousand birds perched on the middle branches of the big trees. They just sat and stared at him, all those blue eyes turned in his direction, and he blinked back at them. The screeching had stopped and there was only the sound of a gentle breeze rustling the leaves.

Joe wondered who and how many were his brothers and his sisters, or maybe his cousins. He tried to talk to them, speaking some of the few words of the only language he knew. He so much wanted to find out who they were and to be their friend.

But they just sat there, staring and silent. No movement, no sound, no greeting, just the faint smell of sulphur coming from the volcano.

He felt like a stranger. This was not his home. These were not his brothers and sisters or they would surely have talked with him and made him feel welcome. Instead, he suddenly felt lonely and very sad.

With a sigh and a powerful flap of his wings, Joe lifted himself from the branch and flew upwards towards the sunlight. The movement of his wings was the

only sound above a silent forest as he turned and flew

back towards Wangaramut.

Joe followed the same flight-path back to the plantation, across the township and out over the hills leaving Rabaul and mixed feelings behind him. He

never looked back. Why was it, he wondered, that his search had not gone as he had hoped? Now he may never know what it was to "be family" among his own kind.

As Joe changed course to follow the coastline south

there was a rumble of distant thunder. Looking ahead he could see the grey shadow of the first afternoon storm sweeping across the coast. It looked as if he was in for a wet arrival. He decided to fly lower so that he could see the land more clearly.

By now the rain was falling steadily, but Joe flew on along the coastline. He was not going to be stopped by a storm. In five more minutes he could see Wangaramut and the familiar foreshore, the tall coconut palms bowing outwards from the beach as if they were welcoming him. The rain was heavy now

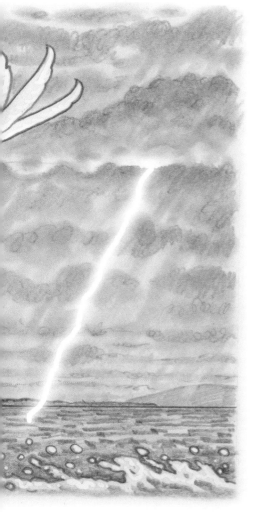

and Joe was already very wet and wind-blown, but he had managed to reach the homestead in good time and in good shape. As he glided over the beach towards the grassed bank, a feeling of great warmth began to spread through him. His mission had ended but a new life had begun. Wangaramut was his home now and its people were his family. Bessie, Toby, Olga, Kamu and yes, even the cranky old Marus. Why hadn't he recognised this before?

Joe landed softly on the back lawn. He was wet but

not weary from the longest flight of his life. As he strutted across the grass, he made up his mind to be friends with everyone at Wangaramut, even the dogs. He would no longer sneak up behind them when they were asleep and tweak their tails.   He would stay clear of silly old Marus and stop pulling out his new

cuttings from the ground. From this moment on, he would be a new bird, a better bird.

He waddled into the living room. Bessie was already home from her visit to Rabaul.

"Hello, Joe, where have you been?" she said, picking him up. "I've been looking everywhere for you."

Joe said "hello" and, then, "cocky kai kai," as he climbed up her arm and onto her shoulder, snuggling into her neck. He was hungry and now he felt tired. If only she knew that he, too, had been to Rabaul. But his mission was over and best forgotten. It had been a long, long day and now he was home with his family – and the happiest ever bird alive!

EPILOGUE

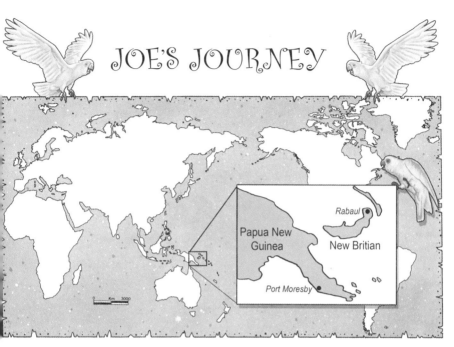

JOE'S JOURNEY

Rabaul

Papua New Guinea

New Britian

Port Moresby

Wangaramut Plantation, New Britain, 1960

The Aftermath

Joe was a special bird in more ways than one because his species (*Cacatua ophthalmica*) normally only inhabited the remote jungles of New Britain. So it was perhaps not surprising that his introduction to living with human beings would lead to more adventures of a rather different kind.

First, he was joined by another Blue-eyed Cockatoo – a female appropriately named Josephine who soon also became part of the Wangaramut lifestyle. The new pet would be good company for Joe, Bessie said.

Then in 1965, five years after Joe's earlier adventures as already related, the Donald family – including Toby, Olga and Bessie – left New Britain to begin a new life on Queensland's Gold Coast. For Toby, his retirement ended a lifetime's association managing plantations in New Guinea and the Solomon Islands.

Bessie with Joe at Wangaramut Plantation, 1960

Before the family moved to Australia, Toby had arranged to give Joe and Josephine to a veterinarian acquaintance in Rabaul, on the condition that

68

the birds were kept in a large aviary. It was a brief next-episode in Joe's life because, early in 1966, an English ornithologist visiting New Guinea arranged with the vet for both birds to be included in a batch of five Blue-eyed Cockatoos to be taken to England's Chester Zoo, centre of the prestigious North of England Zoological Society. Existing zoo records show that the five birds arrived at Chester in March 1966. Three of the birds were female, one was of unknown sex and the fifth was a male This was the zoo's

A big crowd gathering at the entrance to Chester Zoo.

first importation of the rare species which began an important European breeding programme.

Either as a couple, or individually paired with other birds introduced later, Joe and Josephine were almost certainly two of the leading contributors to the initial success of the zoo's breeding programme.

Over the ensuing years, the programme led to a growing "family tree" of Blue-eyed Cockatoos across Europe and beyond, no doubt some of them direct descendants of Joe. Though not all survived, some 48 chicks were hatched at Chester between 1973 and 2001 and birds bred there were sent freely to other collections. These included Rode Bird Gardens, Paignton Zoo, Paradise Park at Hayle,

Dr Roger Wilkinson.

Newquay Zoo, Belfast Zoo, Decin Zoo in the Czech Republic, Berlin Zoo and Walsrode Zoo in Germany, Rotterdam Zoo in the Netherlands, Umgeni Bird Park in South Africa and Loro Parque in Tenerife-Canary Islands, as well as a trusted, leading private breeder in France. The largest holder and most consistent breeder is now Loro Parque.

Dr Roger Wilkinson, then the Curator of Birds at Chester who headed the original breeding programme (he still acts as Blue-eyed Cockatoo Studbook-keeper) says that the birds in the wild are now a threatened species. He predicted their vulnerability after visiting their natural habitat in 2001. "The Blue-eyed Cockatoo is a lowland forest species and, on New Britain as elsewhere, the forest is being replaced by plantations for palm oil," he explains. "The important message now

Blue-eyed Cockatoo chick, hand-reared at Chester Zoo.

70

is to ensure sufficient lowland forest remains to hold viable populations of Blue-eyed Cockatoos and other lowland forest endemics."

While Bessie never saw Joe again after the family moved to Australia, her elder sister, Wendy, made a point of visiting Chester Zoo and enquiring about the birds during an overseas holiday in 2000. There she was shown a large cage in which was one of the original cockatoos. Ignoring zoo staff advice not to get close to the bird – because she was told it was "not too friendly" and could bite – she began talking to it in Pidgin English and making a familiar "clucking" sound she and Bessie had used with Joe many years before at Wangaramut. "He came straight to me and cuddled into my neck," she recalled. "It made me feel so sure it was our Joe."

Bessie's sister Wendy with the Blue-eyed Cockatoo, believed to be Joe, at Chester Zoo in 2000.